Dear Parent:
Your child's love of reading

Every child learns to read in a different wa[...]
speed. Some go back and forth between reading levels and read
favorite books again and again. Others read through each level in
order. You can help your young reader improve and become more
confident by encouraging his or her own interests and abilities. From
books your child reads with you to the first books he or she reads
alone, there are I Can Read Books for every stage of reading:

SHARED READING
Basic language, word repetition, and whimsical illustrations,
ideal for sharing with your emergent reader

BEGINNING READING
Short sentences, familiar words, and simple concepts
for children eager to read on their own

READING WITH HELP
Engaging stories, longer sentences, and language play
for developing readers

READING ALONE
Complex plots, challenging vocabulary, and high-interest topics
for the independent reader

I Can Read Books have introduced children to the joy of reading
since 1957. Featuring award-winning authors and illustrators and a
fabulous cast of beloved characters, I Can Read Books set the
standard for beginning readers.

A lifetime of discovery begins with the magical words **"I Can Read!"**

Visit www.icanread.com for information
on enriching your child's reading experience.

Library of Congress Catalog Card Number: 2021945752

ISBN 978-0-06-315891-7

Book design by Elaine Lopez-Levine

21 22 23 24 25 LSCC 10 9 8 7 6 5 4 3 2 1 ❖ First Edition

I Can Read!

BEGINNING READING 1

BABY SHARK'S BIG SHOW!

pinkfong

Yup Day

Adapted by Steve Foxe

HARPER

An Imprint of HarperCollinsPublishers

Baby Shark loves to try new things.

Daddy Shark does not.

4

Daddy says nope to almost everything.
When he was a kid, he never tried
candy kelp or rode a scooter.

"We should have a Yup Day!"

Baby Shark says.

"On Yup Day,

you say yes to everything!"

Daddy Shark doesn't like

the sound of Yup Day.

But Baby grabs him by the fin.

Baby is going to show him

how great Yup Day can be!

Down in Carnivore Cove,

Baby Shark and Daddy Shark

run into William and his mom.

His mom is a news reporter.

She's looking for
the next big story.

Baby Shark tells her all about Yup Day.
But Daddy Shark is still having
trouble saying yup.

Baby Shark tries changing
his dad's mind by teaching him
a catchy Yup Day song!

When Daddy Shark finally gives in to
saying yup, the whole town celebrates.

Daddy Shark's change of heart
is all over the news.
Mommy, Grandma, and Grandpa
can hardly believe it!

Mommy Shark is glad Daddy Shark
is having fun.

But she is getting worried.

It's good to try new things, but you
can't say yup to everything!

Back in town, Baby Shark is putting

Yup Day to the test.

"Look at this hill," he says.

"It's the perfect place to learn

how to ride a scooter."

Daddy Shark takes a big breath.

"Yup!" he says.

Then down the hill he goes!

"Ahh!" Daddy Shark screams.

He narrowly avoids two kids,

crashes through a picnic, and then . . .

. . . sticks a perfect landing!

Everyone in town

is inspired to say yup!

Two fish say yup
to helping an old lady.
But they end up fighting
over who said yup first!

18

Another fish says yup to a pottery
class when she should be flying
a rocket into space!
Yup Day is getting out of hand.

Daddy Shark can't stop saying yup!

He sees Hank with his pet rock, Rocky.

Daddy says yup to walking Rocky.

He also says yup to buying

a giant can opener.

When the astronaut doesn't show up,
he says yup to flying the rocket ship.

Baby Shark is worried.
Daddy flying a rocket ship doesn't
sound like a good idea.
But this isn't Nope Day!

"Are you sure he can do this?"

Baby Shark asks the commander.

"He's fine," he replies.

"He has a copilot."

Baby Shark sees that his copilot is . . .

. . . the pet rock!

Now Baby Shark is really worried.

He can't let Daddy Shark get hurt.

He's got to stop this launch!

Daddy Shark is worried.

He pushes all of the buttons.

He even breaks the steering wheel!

Baby Shark rushes into the rocket.

He is going to save his dad!

But it's too late.

The ship blasts off!

Daddy and Baby are scared.

"Ahh!" they both scream.

Just then, Baby Shark remembers
the giant can opener.

27

Baby Shark uses the can opener
to cut through the ship.
"You genius!" Daddy Shark says.

With the help of a jellyfish parachute,
Baby Shark and Daddy Shark make a
safe landing down below.

Mommy Shark is happy that Daddy and Baby are safe.

"Does this mean you'll go back to saying nope all the time?" Baby asks Daddy Shark.

"Saying nope to everything is just as silly as saying yup to everything," Daddy says.

"So . . . ice cream for dinner?"
Baby Shark asks.

Daddy Shark smiles.

"Yup!"